## Disney Adventures ④

# CASEBUSTERS

## Check in to Danger

# Disney *Adventures* ④

# CASEBUSTERS

## Check in to Danger

By Joan Lowery Nixon

Disney PRESS

New York

Happy reading, Sean and Brian Quinlan —J.L.N.

Printed in the United States of America.

1  3  5  7  9  10  8  6  4  2

Library of Congress Catalog Card Number: 94-71794
ISBN: 0-7868-3049-2 (trade)/0-7868-4026-9 (pbk.)

Reprinted by arrangement with Disney Press.

WHEN BRIAN QUINN climbed out of the swimming pool at the Piney Point Resort Hotel, Jennifer Hicks smiled sweetly and held out an ice-cream cone. "Here," she said. "It's on the house. That's the good side of my dad's job as manager of the Piney Point."

"Good side?" Brian said. "I hope there aren't any bad sides to the job."

He sat down next to Jennifer Hicks in one of the lounge chairs at the side of the pool and took a mouthful of the ice cream, which was melting fast. Jennifer, like Brian, was thirteen; he liked her big blue eyes and her friendly smile. He had met her earlier that afternoon. She had been standing in the lobby when he and his mom and his nine-year-old brother, Sean, had checked into the hotel. It didn't take long for Brian to introduce himself.

"Well," Jennifer said, "it's kind of strange living in a hotel with people all around, instead of in a house. But most of the time that's okay. It's just that . . ."

She hesitated, and Brian said, "It's just what?"

"Well, sometimes the hotel has . . . problems. In February the main heating unit broke down and a convention group got out of hand and started smashing things. Dad always handles the problems, but it upsets him, and that makes Mom unhappy." Jennifer sighed. "Now there's a problem Dad can't fix, and it's been going on for more than three months."

"That's terrible," Brian said. Jennifer looked

so concerned, Brian took her hand to comfort her. That's when he realized that his hand was sticky with melted ice cream. "Oops," he muttered, and blushed. He pulled his hand away quickly and wiped it on his wet bathing suit. "Uh, what kind of problem is it?" he asked, hoping Jennifer hadn't noticed the sticky mess.

"Thefts from the hotel's kitchen," Jennifer answered, "but not from hotel guests. We're sure that the thief has to be someone who works at the hotel or has access to it, because the thefts have been going on for so long."

"The police are on the case, aren't they?" asked Brian.

Jennifer shook her head. "The hotel has a security chief," she said. "His name is Mr. Otis. But we don't have a police department out here. The nearest town is about five miles away, and it has a sheriff. Each time there's been a theft, he's come out to investigate, but so far he hasn't been able to discover who the thief is. Mr. Otis hasn't had any luck, either."

At that point Sean climbed out of the pool and rubbed his dripping hair with a towel. "Hi, Jennifer," he said, but he laughed when he looked at his brother. "You're wearing an ice-cream mustache, Brian. Here. Have a wet towel." He flipped his towel at Brian.

Brian's face grew hot with embarrassment, but he caught the edge of the towel, jerked it away from Sean, and wiped off his face and hands. "Little brothers can be real pests," Brian mumbled.

"Not Sean," Jennifer said sweetly. "I think he's cute."

"Cute?" Brian grinned wickedly at his brother. "Yeah, maybe he is kind of cute."

"Cut it out!" Sean muttered.

"Sorry, Sean," Jennifer said. "I was just teasing."

But Brian said, "Maybe I can help solve the

problem of your hotel thefts, Jennifer. I'm not a licensed private investigator yet, like my dad, but I've solved a lot of important cases."

Sean threw him a sharp look, so Brian quickly added, "With some help from Sean."

Jennifer perked up. "Your dad's a private investigator?"

"Yes," said Brian, "but he's not here. He's working on a case back home in Redoaks, California. Mom's on the committee putting on the artists convention that's here all week, so she brought Sean and me with her."

No doubt about it, Brian thought, the Piney Point Resort Hotel was a great place for a relaxing vacation. The sun shone bright and warm, and the Oregon air was crisp and fresh and carried the scent of the ocean, which lay just beyond a row of hills.

But this was a case he and Sean might be able to solve on their own. What could be better?

he thought. I want to try, Brian decided. Besides, it looked like Jennifer really needed his help.

"How about it, Jennifer? Will you give us a chance to solve the case?"

## 2

W E'RE ON VACATION, Brian, remember?" Sean complained. "And this case sounds like it could involve a lot of hard work."

Brian tried to look solemn. "I don't mind all the hard work, if it will help Jennifer," he said.

Sean made a gagging face and rolled his eyes.

Jennifer raised an eyebrow. "Brian, do you really, honestly think you can solve a case that the authorities haven't been able to solve?"

"We've done it before," Brian said.

Jennifer glanced at Sean. "Is Brian kidding, or is what he says really true?"

"Brian's telling the truth," Sean said. "We've helped my dad on some of his most difficult cases. We broke up a gang of burglars, and we even caught a guy pretending to be Bigfoot."

"Neat," said Jennifer.

Sean laughed. "Besides, Jennifer, if Brian wants us to work on your case, there's no way you're going to be able to talk him out of it."

Jennifer's eyes sparkled. "If you take the case, can I help?"

"Are you hiring us?" Brian asked.

"How much will it cost?"

Sean gave a bounce. "How about a thousand dollars?"

"No charge," Brian said. "We'll be glad to do what we can."

"You're hired!" Jennifer said.

Brian smiled. "Then okay. You can help us."

"I don't think she should, Brian," Sean blurted out. "She's not an experienced investigator, like us." Girls, Sean thought. Yuck! Then he made a face at Brian.

Brian ignored him. "Just one thing, Jennifer. Grown-ups think that kids don't know what they're doing. So if you tell your parents, they might keep us from investigating. We'll have to keep the case strictly between the three of us. Okay?"

"Okay," Jennifer said.

"We'll change clothes and meet you at that garden behind the hotel in fifteen minutes," Brian told her.

By the time Brian and Sean changed and returned, Jennifer had already settled on a bench in a shady spot under a tree. She greeted them eagerly.

From a pocket in his shorts, Brian pulled out the notebook and pen he always carried with him. "Okay," he said to Jennifer. "Let's get some basic information. What kinds of things have been stolen?"

"Meat," she said.

"You mean like hot dogs and hamburgers and stuff?" Sean asked.

"No," Jennifer said. "I'm talking about huge and very expensive roasts and hams and packages of steaks. It's like the thief keeps getting more and more greedy and more sure he'll get away with it."

"Well, we know one thing for sure," said Sean. "The thief is definitely not a vegetarian!"

Brian frowned. "Be serious, Sean."

"Okay," he said. Boy, Sean thought, Brian was turning into such a grouch! And all on account of Jennifer Hicks. "I don't get it," Sean said. "Why would anybody want to steal so much meat?"

"To sell it," Brian answered. "Isn't that right?" he asked Jennifer.

Jennifer nodded. "And, as I said before, the thief is probably someone who works at the hotel."

"I'm guessing that the thief is reselling the meat to another hotel," added Brian. Jennifer nodded again.

"Do the people who work at the hotel live here?" Sean asked.

Jennifer shook her head. "No. Only Dad, Mom, and me. We have an apartment on the second floor, but most of the other employees live in town."

Sean jumped to his feet. "Solving this case is going to be easy," he said excitedly. "All we have to do is watch the employees when they leave, and if one of them is carrying a big package, we can open it." He waved his arms. "Ta-da! And find a ham!"

"You're the ham," Brian said. "Sit down and stop jumping around."

"Sorry, Sean," Jennifer said, "but your idea won't work."

Sean plopped onto the bench. "Why not?" he asked.

"The hotel has an electronic security system and four security guards," Jennifer explained. "Every single one of the employees, including the guards, must check in and out at a desk by a special door and pass through a metal detector."

"Meat wouldn't set off a metal detector," said Sean.

"You're right," said Jennifer. "But it would be very bulky, and everything an employee takes out of the hotel is examined."

"Everything?" asked Brian. "What about bags and purses?"

Jennifer nodded. "All purses have to be made of clear plastic so that the contents can be seen. The security check was the sheriff's idea because a lot of big hotels—even department stores—use it. But it hasn't helped a bit in stopping the thefts or finding the thief."

She sighed. "Our hotel's chief of security, Mr. Otis, is going crazy because even though he keeps someone on his staff in and around the kitchen area, he can't find out who's stealing the meat or how it's being taken out of the hotel."

"Good surveillance," Brian said, and made a note. "Tell me, what's the sheriff been doing?"

"He went over the personnel files with Dad, took some fingerprints from the meat lockers, questioned some of the employees, and checked records. He comes out every time Dad calls him about another theft, but he can't figure out what the thief's doing, either."

"It's called the MO," Brian said, and explained. "Modus operandi. It means the thief's method of operation."

"Wow!" Jennifer said. "You sound so professional, Brian."

Sean made another gagging face, but Brian ignored him. "I may have the answer to part of the problem," he said. "I remember that Dad once told me about a hotel where food was being stolen from the kitchen. Two employees were wrapping up big roasts and hams and throwing them out with the day's garbage into the trash bins outside. Then when they left, late at night, they'd pull their food packages out of the trash and drive off with them. They sold the meat to a restaurant owner who was more interested in getting a good bargain than in being honest." Brian smiled importantly at Jennifer. "What we need to do is keep watch tonight near the trash bins."

"I'm sorry, Brian, but that idea won't work, either," Jennifer told him. "Meat thefts have been done that way so often, it's the first thing Mr. Otis looked for."

Sean grinned smugly as Brian stopped looking so important. "Any more questions?" Sean asked.

Brian scowled at him, then turned back to Jennifer. "Do you know what time of day or night the thefts take place?"

"No," she said, "but when one of the cooks notices that something is missing, it's always been during the daytime, never at night."

Brian made another note. "How many people are employed at the Piney Point?" he asked.

"Almost two hundred," Jennifer answered.

"Two hundred!" Sean groaned. "Brian, if we investigate all of them, we'll never have time to go swimming!"

Brian shook his head. "We only need to investigate the people who have access to the kitchen," he said. "Jennifer, besides the hotel employees, who else can get into the kitchen?"

"The people who deliver the food each morning," she answered, "but the sheriff told Dad he didn't see how they could be involved. The meat deliveries are checked to make sure everything in the order is there. The delivery men leave, and the order is double-checked as it's put into the refrigerated meat lockers."

"What about the hotel staff the sheriff questioned?" Brian asked. "Is there any way we can find out their names and why he questioned them?"

Jennifer nodded. "Dad was with the sheriff, and he talked about the interviews with Mom at dinnertime, so I heard it all, too. There's Caesar, the head chef. He had an argument with immigration authorities about his official papers. Immigration suspects that some of Caesar's papers are forged, but it takes a long time to trace records."

"That's very interesting," Brian said. "But that information alone doesn't explain why he would steal meat. We'll have to keep looking." He continued making notes. "Okay," he said finally. "Who's next?"

"Edna Marker," Jennifer said. "She's the day-time hostess for the coffee shop. A few years ago she served a prison sentence for burglary."

Brian looked up, excited. "You're kidding!" he said.

"No, I'm not," Jennifer insisted.

"If she's a burglar," Sean asked, "why would your dad have hired her?"

"It's a second chance kind of thing," Jennifer explained. "Hotels that hire people who have served their sentences or have been paroled get a federal tax break. A few of our other employees are in that program, too."

"Like who?" Brian asked.

"One of the bellmen, a gardener, and a housekeeper, but they wouldn't have an excuse to be in the kitchen area."

"No waiters or cooks or busboys?" asked Brian.

"Yes," Jennifer said. "There was a cook, too, but he quit at least three months ago."

Brian frowned. "Dad always starts his investigations with a computer search. The personnel files are probably on computer. Is there any way we could see them?"

"That's private information," Jennifer said, shaking her head. "We'd never be able to get to them."

"Could you at least make a list of the people the sheriff interrogated?" Brian asked.

"Sure," Jennifer answered. "When the sheriff asked for one, Dad printed out a list of employees who work in the kitchen and restaurants. He has a copy in one of his desk drawers."

"That makes it easy," Sean said.

Jennifer got to her feet and brushed some grass off her shorts. She looked worried. "It's only going to be easy," Jennifer said, "if Dad isn't in his office."

# 3

As BRIAN, SEAN, and JENNIFER walked through the main lobby, they had to weave their way through a crowd of guests waiting to take the hotel van to the airport.

A couple suddenly cut in front of Sean, who was trailing behind Brian and Jennifer. Sean sidestepped to avoid them, lost his balance, and fell over a suitcase. "Oompf!" he grunted.

"Careful!" a voice said.

Sean looked up at a tall young man with dark hair and blue eyes. He was dressed in a hotel uniform.

"I'm sorry," blurted Sean, jumping to his

feet. He was afraid the man would blame him for knocking down the suitcase. He took a quick look at the large dark brown leather suitcase. It looked like a million other pieces of luggage, Sean thought, except for a deep scratch across a top corner.

"Oh no," Sean groaned. "I didn't make that scratch," he protested. "It was already there."

The man smiled and put a friendly hand on Sean's shoulder. "It's okay," the man said as he picked up the suitcase. "Help me get all this luggage into the van," he told a bellman. "I'll be leaving for the airport in a few minutes."

Sean sighed with relief as Jennifer led Brian and Sean down the corridor toward the elevators. "That suitcase was already scratched," Sean said. "Honest. There was a deep scratch across one of the top corners. It wasn't my fault."

"Nobody blames you," Jennifer said. "Jed didn't." Sean looked puzzled, and she explained. "That was Jed Anderson. He drives the hotel van."

Jennifer turned down one hallway, then another, and finally reached the door that led to the hotel's business offices. Inside, a middle-aged woman was seated at a desk. She smiled when she saw Jennifer.

"Hi, Martha." Jennifer introduced Brian and Sean. "Martha Wood is Dad's secretary," Jennifer said. She turned to Martha. "Is Dad in his office?"

Martha shook her head. "No, dear. He was called to the dining room. Is there something I can do for you?"

"It's okay," Jennifer said. "There's something I need in Dad's office, but I know where it is. I can get it myself."

With Brian and Sean right behind her, Jennifer opened a door and walked across the large room to her father's desk.

"Shut the door," she whispered to Sean.

Jennifer quickly found what she wanted. "Here," she said as she held out some sheets of paper to Brian. "This is the short list of employees with their names and addresses."

Brian looked through the sheets. "There are some check marks by a few of the names. Do you know what they mean?"

Jennifer leaned over Brian's shoulder. "Blanca?" she wondered, reading the first name on the list. "I know Blanca. She was one of the cooks, but she quit and moved to California. I remember that the sheriff questioned her. Maybe Dad put the checks by the names of people the sheriff questioned."

Brian quickly thumbed through the pages, writing down seven names, then handed the pages back to Jennifer.

She was in the process of putting the report away when the door opened. Startled, Jennifer looked up and said, "Oh! Hi, Martha."

"What are you doing, Jennifer?" Martha asked.

"Uh," muttered Jennifer, "you don't happen to have a rubber band, do you?"

"Of course I do," Martha said. She glanced at the desk drawer and frowned. Then she looked back at Jennifer. "If a rubber band is all that you wanted, you should have asked me."

Martha waited while Brian, Sean, and Jennifer filed out of Mr. Hicks's office. Then she firmly shut the door and handed Jennifer a rubber band from her own desk.

Jennifer smiled as she pulled back her hair and caught it into the rubber band.

"Wow," said Sean once they were out in the hall. "That was close."

"I wonder how much Martha overheard," Brian whispered.

"I don't think we have to worry about Martha," Jennifer said. "She's worked for Dad for years. I don't think she could have had anything to do with the thefts."

Brian, Sean, and Jennifer settled into rockers on a far end of the long porch that stretched across the back of the hotel. "Maybe Martha does have something to do with the thefts," Brian said. "There was a check next to her name."

"Martha?" Jennifer's eyes widened in surprise. "The sheriff talked to Martha, but I thought it was because she's Dad's secretary and knows most of what's going on in the hotel."

"She wouldn't have any reason to be in the kitchen, would she?" asked Sean.

"She thought she did while her nephew worked here," Jennifer explained. "His name is Robert Hopkins."

Brian flipped through his notebook until he found the page on which he'd copied the names. "There was a check by his name, too."

"Robert used to be a cook here at Piney Point, but he quit a week before the thefts began to take place and took a job as a cook in the Empire Hotel in town. Martha was always dropping by the kitchen to see how Robert was doing. I think it bugged him that she was always checking up on him."

"No wonder he went to work someplace else," Sean said.

"I wonder why his name's on the list," Brian said.

"There's something you need to know about Robert," Jennifer said. "He's the cook I told you about who was hired under that federal program for parolees. That's one reason why. Martha worried about him a lot. Another reason is that he's got a short temper. He got into a couple of loud arguments with one of the other cooks and almost got himself arrested when he got into a fistfight one night in town. I think she's scared he'll get into trouble again and go back to prison."

"You're sure he wasn't here when the thefts

took place?" Brian asked.

"I'm sure," Jennifer answered.

"How many other names do we have?" Sean asked Brian. "Not many, I hope."

"Right. Not many," Brian told him. "Besides Caesar, Edna Marker, Martha, and Robert Hopkins, there were check marks next to Palmer Jones, Alice Dunn, and Albert Marts."

"Albert was a gardener at the Piney Point, but he moved to Washington," Jennifer said. "And last month Alice took maternity leave."

"Who's Palmer Jones?" Brian asked.

"Palmer's a waiter, and he's a lot of fun," Jennifer answered. "He always signs up for the employee talent shows and puts on an act with his dog."

"Is he part of that federal program?"

"I don't think so. When Dad told Mom about the others, he didn't mention Palmer."

"Why don't we just ask the sheriff what the check marks mean?" Sean suggested.

"We can't," Brian said. "If the sheriff hasn't been able to solve the crimes, he'd never believe that a bunch of kids could. He'll tell us to keep our noses out of it, and that will mean the end of our investigation. We'll have to figure out those check marks without any help from the sheriff."

They thought a moment before Jennifer said, "I don't know why the sheriff would suspect Palmer. He's a real friendly guy who's nice to everybody. Not many people made friends with Robert while he was here because he's a tough guy with a mean temper. But Palmer did."

"Just because somebody's nice doesn't mean he isn't a thief," Sean said.

Brian agreed. "We've got a lot of stuff to work out. We know what is being stolen and where. What we have to find out is when and why and how. When we learn the answers to those questions, we'll be able to figure out who. That's how private investigators work," he said, smiling at Jennifer. "And at the moment, it seems to me that the big question is how the thief is getting the stolen items out of the hotel."

Jennifer beamed. "You sound like you really know what you're doing as an investigator, Brian."

"It's all part of the job," Brian said.

Sean thought he was going to be sick from all their smiling at each other.

"We'll start with Plan A," Brian said. "We need to find out as much as we can about the employees with the check marks next to their names."

"Then what?" Sean asked.

"We'll go to Plan B. We'll check out the kitchen layout and find out exactly who goes in and out of there."

"When should we start?" Jennifer asked.

"Not now, I hope," Sean said. "It's almost

time for dinner."

Brian grinned. "Haven't you ever heard of combining business with pleasure? We'll be eating in the restaurant, and I can't think of a better place to begin asking questions."

# 4

A SHORT TIME LATER, as the Quinns got ready for dinner, Sean said, "Mom, we wouldn't have to dress up and could just wear our bathing suits if we ate dinner in the Hamburger Hut next to the pool."

Mrs. Quinn put on a pair of pearl earrings and smiled at Sean. "The Hamburger Hut for lunch, the restaurant for dinner, and no arguments. I made reservations, and we've only got five minutes to get downstairs. Let's go. Now."

In the restaurant Mrs. Quinn gave her name to the hostess. "By the way," Brian asked the hostess, "which waiter is Palmer? Jennifer Hicks told me about Palmer's dog act, so I just kind of wondered who Palmer was so I could ask him about his dog."

The hostess smiled. "I'll put you in Palmer's section, and you can ask him all the questions you want."

The Quinns were seated at a table near the window, and almost immediately a young man with sun-bleached hair and a wide smile stepped up.

"Hi," he said. "I'm Palmer. I'm your waiter for tonight. If you'd like your dinner charges added directly to your hotel bill, you can give me your name and room number now. And I'll take your order for drinks."

"Thank you," Mrs. Quinn said.

As she gave him the information, Brian took a long, thorough look at Palmer. Just as Jennifer had said, he seemed like a nice guy. But the sheriff had put a check by his name, Brian thought. He must have had a reason. Brian remembered what Jennifer had told him about Palmer's friendship with Robert Hopkins. Maybe that's why the sheriff had put a check mark by his name, he decided. Brian recalled that last year at Redoaks High School one of the guys in his class had been called to the principal's office after his best friend had been caught spraying graffiti. Because the two boys were friends, the principal thought they were probably in it together. It wasn't exactly fair to make the assumption, but it was information that couldn't be ignored, either.

"Wake up, Brian," Mrs. Quinn said. "What do you want to drink?"

"Uh—milk," Brian said. The others ordered drinks as well.

Sean quickly read through the large menu. When Palmer returned with their drinks, Sean ordered pizza, spaghetti, apple pie, lemon meringue pie, and rainbow sherbet.

"Only spaghetti and a salad, Sean," Mrs.

Quinn said. "We'll discuss dessert later."

After Palmer had left, Brian craned his neck, looking at everyone in the room and checking out the people who came into the restaurant.

"Brian, what are you doing? Are you looking for someone?" Mrs. Quinn finally asked.

"Kind of," Brian said. "I was wondering if Mr. Hicks and his wife and . . . uh . . . Jennifer ate their meals in this restaurant."

"Jennifer is Brian's new girlfriend," Sean said.

"Is not!" Brian said hotly.

Sean snickered and made kissy noises.

Mrs. Quinn smiled, then said, "I doubt they would eat here. The Donallys—you know them—who manage the Redoaks Inn have their own hotel apartments, and their meals are sent to their private dining room from the kitchen."

Brian tried to look as though it didn't matter

whether he saw Jennifer or not, but he was disappointed.

When Palmer brought their salads, he said to Brian, "Jeanne, the hostess, said you wanted to ask me about my dog."

"Yes." Brian searched for the right thing to say. He really wasn't interested in Palmer's dog. He wanted to find out more about Palmer.

"I—uh—heard that your dog does tricks," Brian told Palmer. "What kind of a dog is he?"

"Pete's just a mutt," Palmer said. "A friend of mine got Pete from the pound when he was a pup and gave him to me."

"A friend?" repeated Brian. "Was the friend Robert Hopkins?" He knew he'd scored a point when he saw that his question had startled Palmer.

"Do you know Robert?" Palmer asked. Brian thought he sounded nervous.

"No, but I heard you were good friends. I thought maybe he gave you the dog."

"He didn't," Palmer said. "I mean, well, actually . . . the thing is I hardly know the guy." He quickly left the table.

Brian jabbed a fork into a wedge of tomato. Jennifer had said that Palmer had been openly friendly with Robert, he remembered, but just now he had acted as though he didn't want people knowing they'd been friends. Of course, Brian had to admit to himself, with the way Jennifer said Robert had been acting, he really couldn't blame Palmer.

"Psst, Brian," Sean mumbled. "Palmer turned around and stared at you. Don't look. Now he's staring again."

I don't think that Palmer liked me asking him about Robert Hopkins, Brian thought. He pulled out his notebook and jotted down every detail of his conversation with Palmer. He had learned from his dad that being a detective mostly meant gathering information, then seeing how all the bits and pieces added up. So far, there was nothing very important to go on, Brian realized. But at least they'd made a start.

# 5

ON THEIR WAY out of the dining room after dinner Brian pulled Sean back. "Mom," he said, "Sean and I want to look around the hotel. Okay?"

"I thought you might like to go to the employee talent show," she said. "It's in the ballroom and it starts at nine. Since you're on vacation and can sleep in, Sean can stay up for the show."

"Are you going?" Sean asked.

"Sure, with some of my friends from the convention. I took it for granted you'd go with us."

Brian looked at his watch. "It's only a little

after seven. We've got plenty of time."

"All right," Mrs. Quinn said. "I've got to go over the speech I'm giving tomorrow anyway. I'll meet you in the ballroom in time for the show."

Brian watched their mother walk across the lobby before he went to the bank of house phones and called Jennifer. "Can you come down?" he asked. "We're ready to move into Plan B."

After Brian hung up, Sean said, "Do we have to do everything with Jennifer?"

"What have you got against Jennifer?"

"She's a girl."

"That's dumb," Brian said.

"It's the best reason I've got."

"Jennifer's going to be a big help in this case," Brian said. "I'm hoping she can get us into the kitchen. I want to check it out."

In a few minutes Jennifer hurried toward them. Her cheeks were pink with excitement.

"Plan B," she said. "That means we're going to investigate the kitchen."

"And who goes in and out of there," explained Brian. "That's a question you can help us answer."

"Well, let's see," she said. "There are the waiters, and the busboys, and the janitors, and the cooks, of course."

"Anybody else?" asked Brian, "like people from housekeeping or the bellmen or the office help?"

"You mean like Edna Marker?" asked Sean.

"Right," said Brian. "Don't forget, her name was on the sheriff's list, too."

Jennifer frowned. "Well, it wouldn't be impossible for someone like Edna to visit the kitchen, I guess. But they don't belong there, so if any of them showed up there, the staff would remember," she answered. "That was one of the first questions the sheriff asked. And Mr. Otis practically hangs out in the kitchen, trying to discover who's stealing the meat. He would know who didn't belong there."

"Do you think we could talk to Caesar?" asked Brian. "He's one of the people the sheriff questioned."

Jennifer looked doubtful. "We can try," she said. "But the thing about Caesar is that he's always crabby. And he yells at everyone. Even me. But come on. We'll find out."

Jennifer walked down the hall, past the restaurant, until she reached an unmarked door. She opened it, and Brian and Sean followed her down a corridor that led to the kitchen.

When they reached the kitchen door, she opened it quietly and carefully. Brian and Sean stood with her in the doorway, watching the busy movements of the cooks, waiters, and busboys.

"Which one is Caesar?" Sean whispered.

A cook, wrapped in a white apron, stopped

in front of them. "Hi, Jennifer," said the cook, Ann Smith. "You know that you and your friends don't belong here."

"We're not coming in, Ann," Jennifer told her. "We're just hoping to see Caesar. Is he here?"

"No, he's not," Ann said. "Around six o'clock he said he wasn't feeling well and left to go home."

Brian took a step forward in order to view as much as he could of the large kitchen area.

"Is there something I can help your friend with?" Ann asked Jennifer.

"This is a big kitchen," Brian said, trying to sound casual. Maybe if he could convince the cook that he was just a curious kid she wouldn't get suspicious. "Where are the meat lockers?"

"They're in a back room." Ann gave a wave toward the left where Brian could see a wide door leading to another room.

"Do you have to go through the kitchen to

get to the lockers, or is there another entrance?"

"All deliveries to the meat locker are made through special sliding doors to the dock outside, but those doors are kept locked at all other times," Ann said. "The door over there is the one the cooks use."

She put her hands on her hips and studied Brian. "Why are you asking so many questions?"

"Uh—just interested," Brian said, smiling innocently. "I've never seen a big hotel kitchen before."

"We're very busy right now," Ann said, "especially since we're a little shorthanded because of the employee talent show."

"But that's not until nine," Sean said.

"The people in the show have got to get ready," Ann told him. "Some are wearing costumes, and one of the waiters has to go through a few tricks with his dog to get him warmed up."

"That's Palmer," Jennifer said, "and his dog, Pete."

"Right," Ann said, and smiled. "Palmer brought his dog with him before he went on duty this evening. He put Pete's crate on the loading dock. Before the restaurant opened for dinner, Palmer took us outside and showed us some of Pete's new tricks. Pete's so cute. We even save bones for him."

She suddenly glanced toward the double swinging doors that led to the restaurant. "Oh no! Here comes Mr. Otis again, probably for another look around. I have to get back to work," she said. "Go to the talent show and see Palmer and Pete. They're good."

As Ann reached out and shut the door, Sean said, "If you're through asking questions, Brian, why don't we go swimming?"

"I'm not through asking questions," Brian told him. "I have one for Martha Wood. Besides, it's getting dark."

"By this time Martha's left for the day," Jennifer said. "The pool's lighted at night, and the water's still warm. I vote with Sean. I think we should go swimming."

"Okay, Jennifer," Brian said, "but I'm going to keep asking questions. I've even got a couple for you."

W HEN THEY MET at the pool, Brian sat next to Jennifer on the lounge chair, but Sean threw his towel down on a table and cannonballed into the pool with a big noisy splash.

As he surfaced and hoisted himself to the edge of the pool, he was disappointed that even though Brian and Jennifer had been splashed, they didn't seem to notice. They were too busy making smiley faces at each other. I hope I'm never like that, groaned Sean to himself.

Brian picked up the notebook and pen that he had laid on top of his folded towel.

"Do you always have those with you?"

Jennifer asked.

"Always," Brian said. "They're an investigator's most important tool."

"Big investigator," Sean said disapprovingly as he climbed out of the pool, but Brian ignored him.

"I've been so curious, Brian," Jennifer said. "What are all these important questions you're going to ask me?"

"Probably, 'Did you commit the crime?' and 'Will you confess?' " joked Sean.

"My questions are about Martha Wood and her nephew," Brian answered. "Martha doesn't have a police record, too, does she?"

"Oh, no," Jennifer said. "She's worked for Dad for years and years."

Sean broke in again. "Dad can find out anything about anybody. He could do a computer check into her background," he said.

Brian frowned. "We can't ask Dad to do it because he'd ask why we want to know, and when we told him he'd tell us to stop investigating because he's not here to make sure we don't get into something dangerous."

"Dangerous?" Jennifer asked worriedly.

"If you're scared," Sean said hopefully, "you don't have to help us."

"I'm not scared, and I want to help," Jennifer insisted.

Suddenly Sean looked over his shoulder toward a stand of trees near the Hamburger Hut, which was closed for the night. "Did you hear something weird just now?" he asked. "Like a cough or something?"

"Stop trying to be funny," Brian told him. He turned to Jennifer. "Sure, investigations can be dangerous. If a perpetrator knows you're suspicious of him, there's no telling what he could do. But during any investigation, there comes a time when it's important to go to adults for help. Sometimes we call on Dad, sometimes the police. In this case, if we can get the information we need, we can call on the sheriff."

Jennifer nodded and looked impressed. "When you said perpetrator, you sounded just like the private eyes on TV."

"We—investigators and the police, that is— call them 'perps' for short," Brian told her.

Sean made a face. "There you go again. If Dad heard you bragging . . ." He stopped, listened a moment, then said, "There's that weird noise again, like somebody panting, and I'm not trying to be funny. Didn't you hear it?"

Jennifer frowned and said to Brian, "I don't think Martha would do anything that would be dangerous to us. She's worked for Dad since before I was born, and she's awfully nice."

"She's just one of the suspects," Brian said. "Don't forget Edna, Caesar, and also Palmer."

"And Robert Hopkins," said Sean.

"Right," said Brian. Then he told Jennifer

about his conversation with Palmer in the restaurant.

"But Robert doesn't work here anymore, so what does Palmer being friends with Robert mean?" Jennifer asked.

"That's our job as investigators. We try to find out."

A ruffle of cool air caused Sean to shiver. He reached for a towel to wrap around his shoulders and glanced toward the Hamburger Hut.

"What the—" He jumped. Something had moved in the darkness beyond the circle of lights around the pool.

"Brian!" said Sean. "Somebody is spying on us!"

"Who?" Jennifer gasped.

"Where?" Brian asked, jumping up.

"I saw someone step back behind the Hamburger Hut, but I don't know who it was. It's too dark back there to tell."

The three of them stared at the Hamburger Hut.

"I don't see anybody," Jennifer said.

"Look." Brian pointed at the trees near the Hut. "Those branches are moving in the wind. Could that be what you saw?"

"I don't know," Sean said. "Maybe."

It was Jennifer's turn to shiver. "Why don't we go inside?" she suggested.

"In a minute," Brian said as he jotted down a few sentences in his notebook. "I'm writing what you've told me about Martha to add to what I've written about Palmer. Sometimes just going over the information helps an investigator think of a new line to follow."

He put his notebook and pen on the table and stood up. He looked carefully around the pool area. "I don't see anyone here but us. Come on!" he said, grinning. "Let's go swimming before it gets too cold. Race you to the other side!"

Brian dove into the water. Sean and Jennifer

followed. But before any of them reached the middle of the pool, the underwater lights had suddenly gone out, and the pool was plunged into darkness.

"What happened?" Sean yelled. It was so dark he couldn't even see his hand in front of his face.

"I don't know!" said Jennifer. "It's way too early to turn off the outside lights."

"It's probably just a power failure," said Brian. Then, from the far end of the pool, came what sounded like muffled whispering, then a low growl and a deep chuckle.

"What was that?" asked Sean.

There was a loud splash. Then more heavy splashing.

"Something just jumped into the water with us!" Brian said.

"Something like what?" shouted Jennifer.

"I don't know!" Brian shouted back.

"Yikes!" Sean cried. "Whatever it is it's

swimming right toward us!"

"Oh, Brian," whimpered Jennifer. "What are we going to do?"

"Swim!" yelled Brian. "Swim as fast as you can!"

# 7

NONE OF THEM stopped running until they had reached the back porch of the hotel.

Sean took two deep breaths before he tried to talk. "Brian," he said, "that was close!"

"It sure was," answered Brian. Then he turned to Jennifer. "Has anything like this ever happened before?"

Jennifer's eyes went wide with alarm. "You mean have guests ever been attacked before in the pool? No! Never!"

Brian shook his head. "No. I meant, is it uncommon for the lights to go out like that?"

"The outdoor lights are programmed by computer to go off automatically," she said.

"But the underwater lights stay on all night. Rain or shine."

"Is there a switch for the lights?" he asked.

"Sure," she said, "there's a control panel in a metal box near the Hamburger Hut. But it's locked. Only the head maintenance man would have a key."

"The Hamburger Hut!" echoed Sean. "Brian, that's where I thought I saw someone spying on us!"

"Right," said Brian.

"Do you think whoever was spying on us also turned off the lights?" asked Jennifer.

"It's possible," answered Brian. "The thief might have discovered that we were asking a lot of questions and wanted to know how much we knew."

"But that doesn't explain whatever that . . . thing was in the pool," Sean said.

"I'm not sure exactly," said Brian.

"It was so dark I couldn't see anything,"

Jennifer said. "And with all that splashing, I couldn't hear much, either."

"All that splashing. Hmmm." Brian rubbed his chin. "Sean, why would the thief want to make so much noise if he really meant to harm us?" he asked.

Sean shrugged. "Maybe he just wanted to scare us," he said.

"Right!" agreed Brian.

"But why?" asked Jennifer.

"I think he found out we were asking a bunch of questions about the thefts," explained Brian, "and he wanted to know how much we knew. So he followed us down here to spy on us. Then he decided to try to scare us away. After all, we're just a bunch of dumb kids, right?"

Jennifer wrapped her hands around her shoulders and shivered. "Well, he scared me," she said.

"Jennifer, if you're frightened, you can get

out of this. Sean and I will finish the investigation without you."

"No!" Jennifer tossed her wet hair out of her
face. "I told you before, I'm not scared. And
now I'm mad! I want to help Dad by finding
out who the thief is!"

Sean glanced down at the puddles spread-
ing around their feet. "If we're going to do any
more investigating," he said, "we better find
some towels and dry off."

"Okay," Jennifer told them. "Change clothes
fast and we'll meet in the main lobby by the
elevators in five minutes."

When Brian and Sean returned to their
room, they discovered that their mother had
already left. Brian fished their room key out
of the pocket in his trunks and opened the
door. He and Sean hurried to dry themselves
and get dressed.

Sean was just toweling his hair dry when
Brian suddenly cried, "My notebook! I left it

on the table next to the pool! C'mon, let's go back."

"Go back!" said Sean. "Are you nuts?" But Sean had learned that once Brian had made up his mind to do something, it was no use arguing. He dropped the towel on the bed and followed Brian.

On the way Sean and Brian met Jennifer, and Brian explained about his notebook.

"I'm going back to get it," he said.

"What if whoever was there is still there?" Jennifer asked.

"He had no reason to stay after trying to frighten us," Brian said. "Besides, there's something I want to check out." He opened the door to the hotel's back porch and pointed down the hill. "Look! The pool lights are on again."

But neither Jennifer nor Sean looked convinced that it was safe to go back.

"Why don't you two stay here," said Brian.

"I'll meet you back here in a few minutes." Then he jogged away down the hill toward the pool.

A short time later he came trudging up the hill, carrying their towels.

"I found this on the ground near the Hamburger Hut," he said, holding open his hand. It was the steel lock to the light box, and it was broken.

"Wow!" said Jennifer. "Did you get your notebook?"

Brian sighed and shook his head. "My notebook's gone."

"Uh-oh," Sean said. "The guy who was spying on us might not have been able to hear everything we said. But now that he has your notebook he'll learn what we found out."

"Which is nothing but suspicions so far," Brian said.

"Do you think the thief is going to come after us?" Sean asked. Jennifer gasped.

"Let's not panic," Brian said. "Why don't we check out our suspects and see who could have been here."

"We already know Caesar got sick and went home early," Jennifer said. "And Martha goes off duty at six."

"Then let's find out where Palmer is," Sean suggested.

"He'll be in the talent show," Jennifer said, "and Edna will be, too. She and some of the other employees have a ukulele band."

Brian looked at his watch. "The show's already started. Mom will be wondering where we are. Let's get to the ballroom and see if Edna and Palmer are there."

"Wait a minute," Sean said. "If they are, then whoever was at the pool wasn't one of our suspects."

"Could be," Brian said. "It depends on what time the acts go on. Let's go to the talent show and find out."

As they slipped quietly through the ballroom doors, one of the bellmen was in the middle of his song.

Martha Wood got up from a nearby chair and put a hand on Jennifer's arm. "Sit back here with me," she whispered. "There are some empty chairs."

"I thought you were off duty," Jennifer whispered back.

"I am, but I didn't want to miss the talent show," Martha said.

They sat down, and Sean whispered to Brian, "What if it was Martha at the pool? She's one of the two people you were talking about. She'd have had time to get back here."

A woman sitting in front of them turned and held a finger up to her lips, so Sean settled back and listened.

The bellman received enthusiastic applause, and the announcer introduced Edna Marker and her ukulele band.

Brian murmured to Sean, "So would Edna."

Next, a trio of musicians entertained the audience with some great jazz, and two waitresses followed that act with a tap routine.

Finally, the announcer said, "And last—but certainly not least—we present our popular Palmer and Pete and their assistant, Jed Peterson!"

"Palmer had plenty of time," Sean whispered.

"They all had time," Brian whispered, and leaned forward for a closer look at Pete.

Palmer and Jed ran onto the stage, and Pete—a small black dog—hopped on his hind legs after them. Jed held out a hoop as Palmer bent over. Pete leaped through the hoop onto Palmer's back and balanced again on his hind legs.

Palmer walked slowly across the stage, and Pete ran back and forth between his legs. When they reached the far side of the stage Pete did a double somersault, and the audience broke into laughter.

Jed pulled a table and boxes onstage and built a tower, which Pete climbed. Then Pete sailed through the air into Palmer's arms. The act went on with Pete performing one trick after another, happily wagging his tail at the applause—and the treats he was given by Palmer.

When the act was over, Sean asked, "Do you think that animal in the pool could have been Pete?"

"There's no way of finding out," Jennifer answered.

"Oh yes there is," Brian said. He jumped up when the announcer closed the show and the people in the audience began to leave the ballroom. "Sean, run and tell Mom we were here so she won't go looking for us." He turned to Jennifer. "Come with me. We've got to catch up with Palmer before we're too late!"

B RIAN AND JENNIFER met Palmer as he
came out the backstage door of the
auditorium, his dog on a leash.

Brian bent down to pet Pete.

"Watch out," Palmer said, and tried to pull
Pete back. "Pete's not friendly to strangers.
He bites."

But Brian already had his hands deep in
the thick hair around Pete's neck, and Pete
wagged his tail happily.

Brian stood up and wiped his hands on the
seat of his jeans. He looked Palmer right in the
eyes. "Your dog's still damp," he said.

"I'm not surprised," Palmer answered, and
smiled. "Pete got into some mud, so I gave him

a bath right before the show. That's why we were last on the program."

Palmer tugged on the leash and strode away, Pete trotting to keep up.

"Do you believe him?" Jennifer whispered.

"A good investigator tries to keep an open mind while he's collecting facts and evidence," Brian said. He automatically reached into his pocket for his notebook and was frustrated when he remembered he no longer had one. "In the morning, as soon as the gift shop opens," he said, "I'm going to buy a new notebook."

A short while later, as Brian and Sean got ready for bed, Sean flopped across the end of his bed and waited for Brian to finish brushing his teeth. His mother was already in bed in her connecting room, but she'd told Brian and Sean, "No TV. It's late, so go right to sleep." But Sean was too restless to sleep. He wanted to ask Brian what he'd learned when he'd spoken with Palmer.

From where he lay he could see the hall door to their room. Just then something was slid under the door.

"Yikes!" Sean yelped, and scrambled to his feet.

Brian came out of the bathroom, his pajamas on. "What's the matter with you?" he asked.

"Somebody shoved something under the door!" Sean said.

Brian turned to see what Sean was staring at. "My notebook!" he said.

Brian cautiously opened the door and looked up and down the hall. "Nobody's out there," he told Sean as he shut the door. He locked the dead bolt, then thumbed through the pages of his notebook. "That's funny. Nothing's been changed," he said. "And whoever took it didn't write anything in it. I wonder why he brought it back."

"Maybe he didn't," Sean said. "Maybe somebody else found it, saw your name in it, and brought it back."

"My name isn't in the notebook," Brian said slowly.

"Brian," said Sean, "this is getting really scary."

Brian nodded. Was returning the notebook, he wondered, supposed to be a warning from the thief that he knew who Brian was and could find him whenever he wanted to?

Brian wished he knew.

# 9

THE NEXT MORNING after breakfast Brian called Jennifer. "Let's meet by the elevators," Brian said. "I want to go to the offices and talk to Martha about her nephew, Robert."

On the way downstairs Sean asked, "What about Robert? Jennifer said he didn't even work here when the meat began to be stolen."

"I know," Brian said, "but I keep wondering if there's some connection. That's why I want to find out more about Robert from Martha."

Jennifer was waiting for them as they stepped out of the elevator. "Caesar really was sick yesterday evening," she said. "He called in and said he's got the flu."

"Then he can't be a suspect," Sean said.

"That depends on if he was telling the truth," Brian said.

Sean groaned. "How are we supposed to find out?"

Brian led the way past the guests at the checkout desk. Sean and Jennifer followed.

"Brian, I hope you can solve this case," Jennifer said.

"How about me?" Sean asked.

Jennifer was so busy smiling at Brian she didn't take notice of Sean.

Sean didn't want to stick around and get sick to his stomach watching Brian showing off and Jennifer enjoying it.

"Hey, Brian," he said. "You don't need me to go with you to talk to Martha Wood. I'm going to check out something else."

He waited for Brian to ask what he had in mind, but Brian didn't stop looking at Jennifer.

Shaking his head, Sean turned to go toward

the coffee shop. The lobby was crowded, and he had to step sideways to avoid the bellmen who were wheeling luggage carriers in and out of the hotel. As he dodged around a couple who were hurrying to the front desk to register, he bumped into a large suitcase, knocking it over and falling on top of it. "Yikes!" Sean yelled.

"Are you making a habit of this, little buddy?" Jed Peterson asked. He helped Sean to his feet.

"I'm sorry," Sean said. "I hope I didn't hurt the suitcase."

"No harm done," Jed told him as he picked up the suitcase and swung it to his other hand. The suitcase was old and battered, Sean noticed. And whoever owned it was traveling light, since it had felt almost empty when he had knocked it over.

Jed tucked the suitcase out of the way, next to the bellmen's stand. Then he walked away, busy with his work.

Sean found Edna Marker at the coffee shop. He was curious about Edna because she was an ex-burglar. A middle-aged, slender woman with glasses that kept sliding down her nose, Edna had seated them that morning when the Quinns had gone to the coffee shop for breakfast. Maybe I should hang around the coffee shop and keep an eye on her, Sean had thought. Private investigators spend a lot of time waiting and watching the people they are investigating, he knew. That is an important part of detecting, too.

The small lobby outside the entrance to the coffee shop was filled with chairs and a lot of large potted plants. Edna was talking to Jeanne, the hostess for the dining room, when Sean arrived, so he slipped quietly into a chair behind a broad-leafed palm.

"I've had eight compliments this morning," Edna said. "Our band was pretty good last night."

Jeanne chuckled. "It should have been, with three solid hours of rehearsal before the show. It's lucky we had any strings left on our ukuleles."

Three hours? Sean thought. Forget Edna then. He decided that there was no chance she had been the spy who turned off the pool lights.

Jeanne continued talking. "You're lucky you didn't stick around for the whole rehearsal, Edna. You get so nervous when we make mistakes, and I pulled some bad ones."

Sean perked up. So Edna could have been at the pool! How could he find out what time she'd left the rehearsal?

I'll just ask her, Sean told himself.

A group of people arrived and waited to be seated. Edna led them into the coffee shop, and as Jeanne walked by, Sean jumped to his feet.

"Could I ask you a question?" he said to Jeanne.

Jeanne looked surprised. "Sure. What do

you want to know?"

"Something about your ukulele band rehearsal yesterday," Sean answered. "I heard you say that during rehearsal, Edna Marker left for a while. Do you remember what time that was?"

"I don't know," she said. "It was probably around seven-thirty. Or maybe it was eight."

"Was she gone long?"

"Not too long," Jeanne answered. "Edna said she had a headache because she was hungry, so she left to get an aspirin and something to eat." Suddenly Jeanne looked sharply at Sean. "Why are you asking about the rehearsal and what Edna was doing?"

"So I can tell my brother," Sean said. Without trying to explain, he said, "Thanks for your help," and ran to find Brian.

**10**

SEAN FOUND Brian and Jennifer seated together in one of the wide rockers in the corner of the porch. He told them what he'd learned from Jeanne and said, "So Edna could have been at the pool!"

Brian jotted the information in his notebook. "Jennifer," he said, "just to cover all the bases, could you check with a couple of the others in Edna's ukulele band? Maybe we'll get a better idea of when Edna left the rehearsal and how long she was gone."

"Right," Jennifer said.

Brian turned to Sean. "Let me tell you about Martha. I didn't get anywhere with my questions for her. Jennifer asked her for another rubber band, and while Martha was fishing one out of her desk, I said I'd heard she had a nephew working at the Empire Hotel in town. Her mouth got tight, and she acted kind of nervous and picked up some papers and tried to look busy. So then I said I'd heard that Robert and Palmer were friends. Her face got red, and she told us she didn't have time to talk about her nephew and asked if we wanted anything else."

"She probably doesn't want to talk about her nephew because she's embarrassed that he was in prison," Sean said.

"But Robert couldn't be involved in the thefts because he doesn't work here anymore," Jennifer pointed out.

"Until we have more facts we can't rule anyone out," Brian said. "That includes Robert Hopkins."

"I've got some more information for you to

add to your notebook," Jennifer told Brian. "I was on the dock and watched the meat company unload a delivery early this morning. Mr. Otis was there, too, so I followed him inside and checked the refrigerated meat lockers. There are no locks on the refrigerators, but the doors of the meat locker were locked after the delivery had been made and signed for. That's when Mr. Otis noticed me and told me I didn't belong in the kitchen."

"I've been thinking about the kitchen," Brian said. "The thief has to be someone who's used to being seen in the kitchen. I think both the sheriff and Mr. Otis are overlooking people who are going about their routine business in the kitchen, because they're trying so hard to find someone who doesn't belong there."

"Okay," Jennifer said. "So who are we looking for?"

"I don't know yet. We may have to answer some other questions first."

"Like how the stolen meat gets out of the hotel," Sean said.

"That's the big question," Brian told him, "but right now let's think about something else. We're pretty sure that the thieves sell the meat they steal to restaurant owners who recognize the quality of the meat, want a bargain, and won't ask questions about where it comes from."

Sean broke in. "They couldn't get as much as the meat is worth."

"No, but they'd still get paid pretty well," Jennifer said. "Like I said, those large roasts and hams are really expensive. Some of them cost more than a hundred dollars apiece."

"A hundred dollars?" Sean whistled.

He jumped as he heard his mother say, "There you are!" Mrs. Quinn came toward them, smiling. "My speech went well, and I'm taking a break from all the work I've been doing. How'd you like to go into town with me for a little sightseeing and shopping? You, too, Jennifer."

"Shopping, Mom? Shopping's no fun," Sean said.

"It includes a nice lunch," Mrs. Quinn told him. "I've heard that the Empire Hotel has a lovely big buffet with chicken, roast beef, and ham."

"The Empire Hotel?" Brian said. "That's where Robert Hopkins works."

"Who's Robert Hopkins?" Mrs. Quinn asked.

"Martha Wood's nephew . . . a waiter . . ." Brian hesitated. "Mom, it takes too long to explain," he said. "If it's okay with you, could we skip the sightseeing in town? We've got a lot of stuff to do here."

Mrs. Quinn smiled. "No problem," she said. "One of my conference friends would like to go with me, I'm sure. That's what I like about these conventions. It's a good place to renew old acquaintances and make a lot of new friends. It's like a network of friends."

"That's it! That's the answer!" Brian said.

"What answer?" Mrs. Quinn asked.

"It's kind of a puzzle we're trying to work out," Brian told her, "and the pieces are beginning to fall into place. I'll tell you all about it later, Mom. Have fun in town. We'll see you at dinnertime."

As soon as Mrs. Quinn left, Brian said to Sean and Jennifer, "Come on! Quick! Let's go back to the kitchen. I've got just a few more questions to ask."

# 11

AS THEY REACHED the kitchen and Jennifer opened the door, Ann stopped her work, smiled, and came to meet them, shaking her head. "Here you are again, and you know you're not supposed to be in the kitchen. What do you kids want this time?"

"You said you save bones for Palmer's dog, Pete," Brian asked. "How does Palmer get the bones?"

"Easy," she said. "We keep them in a special section of the meat locker, and Palmer comes to get them whenever it's handy. That way he doesn't bother anybody. As a matter of fact, he was here just a little while ago."

"Does he wrap the bones in aluminum foil?

Or plastic wrap?"

"I don't know what he wraps them in," Ann said. "He always carries them out in that big gym bag of his." She stared at Brian. "What difference does it make?"

"Our neighbor has a dog," Sean piped up.

"Sorry, we don't give out bones to anyone but Palmer," Ann said.

A chef hurried from the back room, his tall white hat quivering. "The steaks!" he shouted. "The entire package . . . delivered this morning! Gone! And a large ham! Now, you tell me—where could they be?"

"What time were they delivered?" Brian asked.

"Out!" Ann said. "You kids don't belong in here!"

She hustled them out quickly and shut the door. In the hallway Brian smiled. "I have a good idea now of who's been stealing the meat!" he announced. "It's like a network of contacts. And it starts with Palmer."

"But security examines Palmer's gym bag when he leaves the hotel," Jennifer said. "They open and look through everything. Just ask Mr. Otis. He'll tell you." She made a face. "Besides, meat would be ruined if it wasn't refrigerated all day long."

"Right," Brian nodded. "I'm not sure yet how Palmer is transporting the stolen stuff from the hotel. Especially since everyone is searched."

"Not everyone," Sean reminded him. "The guests aren't searched."

"Guests," Brian said. "I wonder . . ."

"But the thief can't be a guest," Jennifer said. "Our hotel guests are here for short visits, and the thefts have been going on for more than three months." Jennifer opened the door to the main hallway, which was filled with a tour group lining up at the restaurant.

"We've got to talk about this where we can't

be overheard," Brian said. "Let's try the porch."

But the porch was crowded with guests enjoying the beautiful day, and the garden bench was already occupied.

"If we go to our apartment, Mom's likely to walk in on us," Jennifer said. "But off the lobby there's a small conference room that's probably empty. Come on."

They elbowed their way through the group of people who were signed up to take the airport shuttle, then entered the room and turned on the lights.

Brian said, "Okay. This is how I've figured it out. What Mom said about her network of friends made me think about Palmer and his friends. Palmer takes the meat from the refrigerated lockers and places it in his gym bag, and no one suspects him because everyone thinks he's carrying dog bones. Then Palmer passes the bag to his friend, Jed, who takes the gym bag to the airport."

"But Brian," said Sean. "A gym bag is pretty conspicuous. After a while, wouldn't someone become suspicious of it?"

Brian frowned again and scratched his head. "You're right."

"Besides," said Jennifer, "all employee bags are searched."

"And everyone knows that that's Palmer's gym bag," said Sean. "Also, wouldn't Mr. Otis wonder why Jed was driving Palmer's gym bag to the airport?"

"Right," said Brian, and nodded. "What we're looking for is a big bag that is so inconspicuous that no one in the hotel would notice it going back and forth. Even after a lot of trips."

Trips, thought Sean. Suddenly he remembered the first time he had tripped over the old brown suitcase in the lobby. He hadn't even noticed it there with all the other suitcases. That had to be it!

"Suitcases!" shouted Sean.

"What are you talking about?" asked Brian.

"The meat isn't being carried out in a gym bag," explained Sean. "It's being taken out in a suitcase. No one would pay any attention to a suitcase. They would think it belonged to a guest!"

"That's it!" agreed Brian. "I bet there are hundreds of suitcases that go back and forth each day. And most of them all look alike. It would be hard to notice one from another."

"Yeah," said Sean, "except if it was brightly colored or had a mark or something on it. Most of the suitcases I saw in the lobby were all just kind of boring looking."

"Okay," said Brian. "Jennifer, how many trips does the hotel van make to the airport each day?"

"Four," Jennifer answered.

"So on any one of them Jed could add the suitcase. Then, after he drops off his passengers, he could drive to the Empire Hotel and pass the meat to Robert, who sells it to whoever buys the meat for the hotel."

Jennifer whistled. "It sounds right," she said, "but how are we going to prove it?"

Sean was thinking about what he had said about marks on the suitcase. The word seemed important, but he couldn't figure out why. Then he remembered. The scratch on the suitcase! Both times that he tripped on the suitcase, he noticed a scratch on the top corner—the same scratch!

"Brian!" he shouted. "Remember when I tripped over that suitcase before and worried about scratching it? A little while ago the same old brown suitcase was there in the lobby along with the others, ready to be placed in the hotel van! I saw it! I'll bet those missing steaks are in it!"

"I'll get Dad," Jennifer said. She jumped up and ran out the door, returning in a few minutes with her father.

After Brian and Sean introduced themselves, it took only a few minutes to tell Mr. Hicks everything they'd found out and what they suspected.

"Your ideas make good sense," Mr. Hicks told them.

"Do you think Martha knows about it?" Jennifer asked.

"That's for the sheriff to discover," Mr. Hicks said, "but I doubt that Martha's at fault. I'm guessing that Martha's concerned that her nephew might be involved in our thefts but probably has no idea how."

He smiled as he said, "I can vouch for Edna, too. She came to the offices during rehearsal, asking for an aspirin. Martha gave Edna an aspirin, led her to a sofa in the employee lounge, and tucked her in for a nap."

"I think we'd better call the sheriff," Brian said.

"And the front desk," Mr. Hicks said. As soon as he'd hung up the phone, he said, "Jed has already left with the van. The sheriff is going to let him carry out the delivery and will pick up both Jed and Robert at the Empire Hotel when Robert accepts the stolen meat."

"What about Palmer?" Jennifer asked.

"I was told to have Mr. Otis take Palmer into custody."

"Nobody saw Palmer give the meat to Jed. So how will the sheriff prove that Palmer is in on the thefts?" Jennifer asked.

"Fingerprints!" Sean said. "I bet Palmer will have his fingerprints on the suitcase."

"And a lab might be able to pick up traces of meat in his gym bag," Brian added. "Also, Palmer's the only one of the three who has access to the kitchen." His smile was grim. "I doubt that Jed or Robert will let Palmer go free and take the rap by themselves."

"Take the rap!" Jennifer repeated, her eyes

wide with admiration. "Oh, Brian, you sound just like the private eyes on television."

Brian tried to look modest. "We private investigators have a language all our own," he told her.

"Oh, yuck!" Sean muttered. "Give me thieves, robbers, or ghosts. But please! No more girls!"

Mr. Hicks took a pager from his belt and punched in some numbers. "I'm going to meet Mr. Otis," he said. "Suppose the three of you order whatever you want from the Hamburger Hut while you wait. If all goes as we think it will, I promise you'll be the first to know."

As soon as Mr. Hicks left the room, Brian said, "I want to be there when Palmer's busted, not hear about it later. Don't you?"

"You bet," Sean said.

"Let's go!" Jennifer cried.

Mr. Hicks and Mr. Otis weren't hard to shadow. They strode toward the dining room, so intent on the business at hand that they didn't notice they were being tailed.

Brian, Sean, and Jennifer stopped at the entrance to the nearly empty dining room and watched as Mr. Hicks spoke to Palmer.

Palmer looked shocked and scared. Then he bolted, dashing toward the main entrance to the dining room.

"Stop him!" Mr. Otis yelled.

Palmer was fast, but Sean grabbed a menu and swatted him in the face as he ran through the doorway.

"Ooof!" Palmer gasped, and staggered back a step.

"Ugh!" he grunted as Brian hit him below the knees, knocking him flat.

"Ouch!" he shouted as Jennifer sat on him.

"Good work, kids," Mr. Hicks said as Mr. Otis hauled Palmer to his feet, handcuffed him, and led him away.

Brian grinned. "Wow! This is exciting! Wait

till we tell Dad that we solved another case!"

Solving a case was fine, but Sean was much more excited about what Mr. Hicks said next: "Why don't all of you join me for some ice cream while we talk about a reward?"

**JOAN LOWERY NIXON** is a renowned writer of children's mysteries. She is the author of more than eighty books and the only four-time recipient of the prestigious Edgar Allan Poe Award for the best juvenile mystery of the year.

❪

*"I was asked by* Disney Adventures *magazine if I could write a short mystery. I decided to write about two young boys who help their father, a private investigator, solve crimes. These boys, Brian and Sean, are actually based on my grandchildren, who are the same ages as the characters. My first Casebusters story was a piece about a ghost that haunts an inn. This derives from a legendary Louisiana inn I visited which was allegedly haunted. Later, I learned the owner had made up the entire tale, and I used that angle in the story."*

— JOAN LOWERY NIXON